Anonymous

Memorial of Edward R. Geary, D.D., Late of Eugene City, Oregon

Containing biographical sketches, memorial discourse and tributes of respect

Anonymous

Memorial of Edward R. Geary, D.D., Late of Eugene City, Oregon
Containing biographical sketches, memorial discourse and tributes of respect

ISBN/EAN: 9783337307844

Printed in Europe, USA, Canada, Australia, Japan

Cover: Foto ©Raphael Reischuk / pixelio.de

More available books at **www.hansebooks.com**

MEMORIAL

OF

EDWARD R. GEARY, D.D.

LATE OF EUGENE CITY, OREGON.

CONTAINING

BIOGRAPHICAL SKETCHES, MEMORIAL DISCOURSE

AND TRIBUTES OF RESPECT.

EUGENE CITY, OREGON.
THE OCCIDENT PRINTING HOUSE, 429 MONTGOMERY STREET,
SAN FRANCISCO, CAL.
1887.

CONTENTS.

These Tributes are numerous and varied. The limits of this publication compel a selection, which is made with reluctance. In the following articles, some repetitions will appear that could not be avoided without omissions which would be mutilations in the eyes of the writers, and impose a task upon the editor which he would not willingly assume. Some of these tributes touching the life and character of Dr. Geary, coming, as they do, from men of different callings and culture, yet displaying a remarkable unanimity, are spontaneous and independent estimates of his worth and dignity; and may, therefore, be regarded as the final verdict of his contemporaries.

Numerous letters have been received by Mrs. Geary from eminent gentlemen in different parts of our country, expressing their sincere sympathy for her and their high appreciation of the character and labors of Dr. Geary. These being private and personal, are not inserted in this volume.

SERVICES AT THE FUNERAL.

Died at his residence in the city of Eugene, Oregon, the Rev. Edward R. Geary, D. D., Pastor of the Presbyterian Church, September 1, 1886, in the 76th year of his age.

The public funeral was conducted in the Presbyterian Church in the presence of a great concourse of citizens and visitors from abroad. Appropriate and touching addresses were made by Rev. S. G. Irvine, D. D., of the United Presbyterian Church of Albany, Professor Thomas Condon, of the State University, Rev. A. C. Fairchild, of the Methodist Episcopal Church, Rev. C. M. Hill, of the Baptist Church, and Rev. G. M. Whitney, of the Christian Church.

The profound sympathy felt by the entire community forced expression in many tears; and groups paused long because they knew they should "behold his face no more." The remains were then conveyed to the Masonic Cemetery, where the interment took place after the final funeral ceremonies.

ACTION OF THE SESSION.

Extract from Minutes of the Session of the First Presbyterian Church, Eugene City, Oregon, October 31, 1886.

It is with the profoundest sorrow we have to record the departure to his heavenly home, of our beloved friend and pastor, REV. EDWARD R. GEARY, D.D., who heard and obeyed the summons from his Heavenly Father, September 1, 1886.

During the eleven years of his ministry over this church, one hundred and twenty members were received into communion, increasing the total above dismissals and deaths to ninety-three. When our present church edifice was building, he took a personal interest in its progress, aiding materially with his influence and his means. With liberal hand, he always assisted largely in the benevolent work of the church.

We deem it a pleasure as a Session, voicing as well the thought of the whole church, to bear testimony to his untiring fidelity as a minister of the Gospel, in his kindly work of reclaiming the erring, strengthening the weak and building up the kingdom of Christ among us.

We appreciate highly his faithful and eloquent presentation of Bible truth from the sacred desk which he honored so long and so well, and we venerate his memory as one whom we love for his works' sake.

We record with gratitude, the cordial relations always existing between him and the Session.

Toward the close of his ministry he frequently reverted to the prospect of his having soon to lay aside the growing weight of so large a pastoral charge; and proposed of his own accord, at the end of last year to supply the pulpit as exigency might require, till the church should secure a pastor, seconding heartily every effort of the Session to accomplish the end.

We feel it to have been a blessing to be associated so long, with so large-hearted a man, true and loyal to his Master; and trust and pray that the benediction of his memory may never pass from our church and fireside till we clasp hands about the Great White Throne. Our heartiest sympathy is extended to the bereaved wife and family, recognizing, as we do, the poignancy of the sorrow that has entered their hearts, yet sanctified by the precious heritage of honor, that crowns all our lives through the godly conversation of him who went in and out before us as a true husband, father, and shepherd of immortal souls.

Signed : JOHN STRAUB,
Clerk of Session.

ACTION OF THE BOARD OF REGENTS.

WHEREAS, The Rev. Dr. Edward R. Geary, who was for a long time a Regent of the University of Oregon, has, since our last meeting, departed this life :

Resolved, That in the death of Dr. Geary, the University has lost an ardent and efficient friend and supporter, and the Regents a wise and faithful counselor and co-worker.

Resolved, That a copy of this preamble and resolution, be prepared by the Secretary and sent to the widow of the deceased.

Attest :

JOSHUA J. WALTON,
Secretary.

Adopted June 16, 1887.

OBITUARY NOTICE.

From The Occident, San Francisco, Sept. 8, 1886.

REV. EDWARD R. GEARY, D.D.

This eminent man and minister died at his residence in Eugene City, Oregon, September 1, 1886. He was a graduate of Jefferson College, class of 1834, and his theological course was completed at Allegheny. His early ministry was exercised in Fredericksburg, Ohio, and was very fruitful. He came to Oregon in 1850, authorized by the Board of Education to establish a Christian Academy to be erected in due time into a college, and by the Board of Missions to preach the gospel and gather churches. In conjunction with Revs. Robert Robe and Lewis Thompson, he organized the Presbytery of Oregon in 1851. Dr. Geary prosecuted his ministry while he was employed as Superintendent of Indian Affairs, acted as County Clerk and was afterward appointed Judge. He was compelled to resort to these employments to support his family. Much of his journeying was done on foot, with occasional help on the way, the price of a horse and saddle being equivalent to a year's salary from the Board.

In the pioneer days the missionary work was exceedingly arduous. The settlements were few and distant, and the difficulties of the work were increased by the unwillingness of sectarians to unite in a common organization, and the hostility of men who were opposed to all religion. Notwithstanding these discouragements, the Presbyterian church was established in important places, an academy with a college charter was founded and is still flourishing. Indian tribes were taught and rights defended, and moral reforms set on foot, in all of which Dr. Geary bore a very conspicuous part.

He continued in the active service of the ministry, against repeated inducements to devote himself to other callings. The nomination for Governor of the State he declined, saying to the writer, " I am a minister of Christ, and intend to live and die in his service." He might have been elected United States Senator if he had held his ordination vows with less inflexible grasp.

Dr. Geary was a fine scholar, a well versed theologian, a convincing preacher. He was capable of high philosophical themes, as well as scientific investigations. His mind was powerful, and worked with tremendous force along any line which he pursued. His spirit was devotional, and his ministrations among the poor and the afflicted will never be forgotten.

While his principles were conservative, his sentiments were liberal and generous. He deplored the sectarian divisions of the church, and warmly advocated the open fellowship of all evangelical denominations.

He was highly respected by professional men for his learning and dignity, and by all classes for his benevolence, worth and integrity. He was too manly to stoop to meanness ; too generous to take advantage of an enemy or exact his own; too forgiving to harbor resentment; and his brethren in the ministry ever found him a faithful friend, a wise counselor, and a brother worthy of increasing affection and reverence. There is not a man on the Coast who ever knew Judge Geary or Dr. Geary, that does not mourn his loss.

The death of his daughter, Elizabeth Woodbridge, was a blow from which he did not recover. He resigned his charge last April, but continued to assist the congregation as pastor and in efforts to secure a successor.

To Mrs. Geary and the children of our venerated brother, THE OCCIDENT tenders its heartfelt sympathy, in which we are sure the ministers and churches of both our Synods share.

MINUTE OF THE PRESBYTERY OF OREGON.

With deep and unfeigned sorrow the Presbytery of Oregon is called upon to make a record of the death of Rev. EDWARD R. GEARY, D.D. He died at his home in Eugene, on the 1st of September, 1886.

Dr. Geary was born near Boonsboro, Washington Co., Maryland, April 30th, 1811. His age, therefore, was seventy-five years and four months. His father, who was a man of classical culture, was his principal teacher. His mother was an exemplary Christian. Of her pious care of her children Dr. Geary often spoke.

At the age of thirteen he was employed as an assistant clerk in the office of the Recorder of Westmoreland Co., Pa., and occupied his leisure in gratifying a thirst for knowledge by reading useful books. Being observant and intelligent, he acquired a knowledge of public speaking by listening to the pleas and proceedings at the Court House.

He commenced a course of study in the Academy of Greensburg, Pa., supporting himself by writing in the public offices and teaching. He entered an advanced class in Jefferson College in 1831. His varied preparation gave him a good standing in the college from the start. His religious impressions, made in childhood, had grown strong and decisive; and during his senior year his thoughts were turned to the ministry of the Gospel. His theological course was pursued in the seminary at Allegheny. He has spoken with deep gratitude of his indebtedness to his theological professor, Dr. Job F. Halsey, whose influence he acknowledged only a year or two ago. After a few years spent in Alabama in teaching, he returned to Pennsylvania, and being licensed he was called to the charge of the church at Fredericksburg, Ohio, and was there ordained and installed. Thirteen years of faithful and laborious service were distinguished for unusual success. Frequent revivals brought rich blessings and large ingatherings.

At this time, 1851, the Board of Education and Domestic Missions sent Mr. Geary as a missionary to Oregon. Dr. Van Rensselaer's noble and comprehensive plan of education was undergoing successful experiments; and Mr. Geary was authorized to establish schools or academies under the direction of the Board of Education, and to gather congregations under the direction of the Board of Missions. Although he was not ignorant of the recency of " white " settlements in Oregon, he was not wholly prepared for the wide extent of country which stretched on every side between the settlements, and which was still trodden by roving bands of Aborigines ; and he found that the entire Pacific Northwest was in a great measure unknown, and the general impression respecting it, was vague or erroneous. The object therefore of the Board of Missions could be gained only to a very limited extent ; and the object of the Board of Education, after a few experiments, was necessarily postponed for a larger population.

In the work of Missions and Christian Education, Mr. Geary was ably seconded by his wife, who was a graduate of Mt. Holyoke Seminary, and who belonged to the Woodbridge family, well known in the Eastern States for their ability and culture, as well as for their Christian integrity and influence.

Through innumerable trials incident to the early settlement of every country, intensified in Oregon by the circumstances just referred to, sparseness of population and bitter and destructive Indian wars, our Brother Geary maintained the cause of Christ : but he was compelled, by the necessity that knows no law, to support his growing family by secular pursuits—which was indeed the experience of all the early missionaries on this coast. His service of the government as superintendent of Indian Affairs, enabled him to make wise and salutary improvements in the management, and secured his firm friendship for the poor red men.

He declined important political preferments, and welcomed with great gladness of heart his full return to the work of the ministry in which he performed manifold services without earthly compensation. In conjunction with Rev. W. J. Monteith he founded Albany Collegiate Institute, and labored in it for years as President and teacher while he continued to preach. He was pastor at Brownsville, at Pleasant Grove, and at Albany, until in 1875 he settled in Eugene City, where he continued his labors until last April, when he resigned the pastorate. The illness which terminated fatally was caused by a disorder that was pronounced mortal from the first. We are thankful that he was not compelled to linger a long time, and that he was able to bear testimony to the faithfulness of God, to his unfaltering trust in our Redeemer, and to his unclouded hope of heaven. He was a regent of the University of Oregon in which he performed efficient service. He several times represented his Presbytery in the General Assembly. He received his title Doctor Divinitatis from his Alma Mater, Jefferson College, in 1870. He was one of the constituting members of the Presbytery of Oregon, the other two being the Revs. Robert Robe and Lewis Thompson.

Dr. Geary excelled as an extempore speaker, theologian, debater and counselor. In social life he was genial, sympathetic and influential. In private personal intercourse he was especially attractive and fraternal ; and the more he gave his confidence, the more his best qualities shone forth in the liberality of his sentiments and the affluence of his affections.

But there was nothing clannish in his nature. There was ever a place within the circle of his sensibilities for man as man, and the cry of want or weakness and the mute appeal of sorrow found in him an uncalculating friend and helper.

Dr. Geary held the views called Presbyterian as altogether scriptural and as alone competent to explain the purposes of God in the scheme of salvation and the divine plan in the visible organization of the church. While his loyalty to his own church was firm from intelligent conviction, he embraced all evangelical denominations in the unity of the faith and of the spirit and labored in all catholic causes to build up the Kingdom of God among men, and promote the world's preparation for the coming of her King.

The cast of his mind was philosophical, yet he was endowed with a rich imagination and delicate sensibilities. He could indulge in abstruse speculations, which required the highest analytical powers, and delight in poetic creations of the finest mold ; but he esteemed them all as of little worth unless he could lay them as tributes at the foot of the Cross.

Thus lived and died our beloved and venerated Brother Geary, honored and respected by all classes, and lamented by the entire community. May his memory be cherished as a sacred legacy, that his associates and successors may emulate his excellence.

We express our heartfelt sympathy for Mrs. Geary and the children, and other relations of our departed brother. May his prayers for them be answered, and his labors for the church of Christ be blessed a thousand fold, in the future growth and prosperity of this part of our beloved land.

Ordered to be engrossed on the records, and a copy forwarded to Mrs. Geary.

Attest: J. V. MILLIGAN.
Stated Clerk, Presbytery of Oregon.

PUBLIC LIFE

OF

Edward R. Geary, D. D.

BY THE

Hon. M. P. Deady, LL. D.

Judge of the United States Circuit Court and President of the Board of Regents of the University of Oregon.

PUBLIC LIFE.

THE REV. EDWARD R. GEARY, D. D., spent the last thirty-five years of his life in Oregon. During all this period he was in the ministry of the Presbyterian Church, and engaged more or less in its active duties, as a missionary and otherwise.

But much of this time was given to the discharge of public duties of a useful and important character, in positions to which he was called by the appreciation of his fellow-citizens.

He was a man of marked and varied ability, endowed by nature with a sound mind in a sound body, enriched by a generous education and large experience and controlled by a lively sympathy and kindly interest in whatever concerned the welfare of his kind and country. It was, therefore, impossible for him to refrain from taking an active part in anything affecting the spiritual or worldly welfare of the community in which he lived.

Dr. Geary was sent to Oregon by the Presbyterian Board of Home Missions for the purpose of establishing schools and churches in the country. He arrived here in April, 1851, and soon settled in the immediate vicinity of

Lafayette, in Yamhill County—then the second town in population and importance in the territory.

Here, in conjunction with his wise counselor and faithful help-meet—Mrs. Nancy Woodbridge Geary—he established and maintained for some time, a girls' boarding school, which made its impress for good on those who were fortunate enough to come within its wholesome influence.

From the fall of 1851 until the spring of 1853, he served as clerk of the U. S. District Court, for Yamhill County—his excellent penmanship and natural aptitude for legal forms and proceedings making him an excellent officer.

During this time he held service and preached once or twice on every Sunday at Lafayette and elsewhere in the vicinity. The writer has often heard him in the old court room at that place. Generally his theme was Christian conduct and Gospel truth, but sometimes he turned aside to wrestle with the once awful problem involved in foreknowledge, foreordination and free will.

Early in 1853, he was appointed Secretary to the Superintendent of Indian Affairs for Oregon and Washington, which place he retained until the latter part of 1855. During his secretaryship treaties were negotiated with all the Indian tribes in middle Oregon from the south to the north boundary of the State. They are published in the tenth volume of the U. S. Statutes at large, and Mr. Geary's name is appended to them, as Secretary, and that of Joel Palmer, as Superintendent of Indian

Affairs. In this way he had much to do with shaping the policy of the government towards these Indians and providing for their future education and improvement.

In the fall of 1856, he removed with his family to Linn county and there devoted most of his time to the work of the ministry, in the churches of Corvallis, Calapooia, Brownsville and Diamond Hill; and in 1858 he was elected Superintendent of Schools for Linn county.

Early in 1859 he was appointed Superintendent of Indian Affairs for Oregon and Washington. During his incumbency of the office he was distinguished by a wise and vigorous administration of its affairs. The office was then one of much importance and responsibility financially and otherwise. He was doubtless selected by the President for the place on account of a strong petition which the writer had procured for his appointment to the office in the fall of 1855. In 1861 he resigned the position and returned to his ministerial work at Brownsville, Linn county; where he also materially aided in the erection of a woolen mill, going east in the fall of 1861, to purchase the machinery for the factory.

In the spring of 1865 he removed to his farm near Albany, thence to Albany in the fall of 1868 where he remained until 1875.

In 1866 he was appointed county judge, which office he held for some years. The succeeding years of his residence in Linn county were largely devoted to the establishment of the Collegiate Institute at Albany. He served one year—1868 and 1869—as its President, and as President of the Board of Trustees for a number of years. In 1870, his Alma Mater—Jefferson College, Pennsylvania—conferred on him the honorary degree of Doctor of Divinity. Later, in the year 1884, he had the pleasure and distinction of attending the commencement exercises of the college on the semi-centennial of his own graduation, where he sat down to dinner with the remaining half-dozen of his classmates, among whom was the venerable Dr. Samuel Hamill, the distinguished founder of the Lawrenceville Preparatory School, near Princeton, New Jersey.

During all this time he continued to minister to the feeble churches in his vicinity—furnishing largely his own support.

In 1875, he removed to Eugene and took charge of the Presbyterian church at that place, where he remained until his death on September 1, 1886.

Soon after going to Eugene he was appointed by the Governor one of the Regents of the University of Oregon, then lately established at that place. As Regent he was very useful in helping to plan and conduct the work of this new and important institution, so as to make it an efficient means of higher education in Oregon. His wise counsels and stimulating confidence will be missed in the future management of the school.

Thus living and dying at the advanced age of 75 years, with his faculties unimpaired, Edward R. Geary impressed himself for good, on the opinion and action of this State in a large and lasting measure.

His venerable, but manly form will be seen no more in the gatherings of the people, in the Halls of Learning, or in the House of God, where his voice was wont to be heard in support of material improvement, intellectual progress, and whatever makes for righteousness.

But he has not lived in vain. The effect of his faithful teaching and good example, for more than a third of a century in Oregon, remains with us and will bear fruit for generations to come.

"To him that soweth righteousness shall be a sure reward."

"Blessed are the dead which die in the Lord from henceforth; and their works do follow them."

DISCOURSE

COMMEMORATIVE OF THE LIFE AND CHARACTER

OF THE

REV. EDWARD R. GEARY, D. D. •

ADDRESSED TO

THE CONGREGATION OF THE PRESBYTERIAN CHURCH OF
EUGENE CITY, OREGON

BY REV. A. L. LINDSLEY, D. D.,

*Pastor of First Presbyterian Church, Portland, Oregon, and Professor-elect in the
San Francisco Theological Seminary.*

SABBATH MORNING, OCTOBER 31, 1887.

MEMORIAL DISCOURSE.

"HE BEING DEAD YET SPEAKETH." *

These words relate to one of the first worshipers of the living God. His name is sculptured upon the earliest altar of our race; and reappears with imperishable honor near the last of the inspired writings. The influence of his consecrated life was so benign and salutary, that it has been projected through all ages, and will be felt while time lasts.

His is an unfading example of spiritual worship and acceptable offerings, permanent in their nature, and therefore independent of all changes of climate, culture, or civilization. To well regulated minds it is an inexpressible delight to enjoy the favor of Heaven and the approbation of conscience. But when God makes known his appreciation of one's character, and confirms it by giving in his testimony thereto, it must kindle in the soul of the worshiper a perpetual joy. It must lift him above the earthly entanglement, and bid him soar away at last to his native skies. His body perishes; but his name survives. His tongue is silent ; but his renown is a living voice. "By it he being dead yet speaketh."

---

* By faith Abel offered unto God a more excellent sacrifice than Cain, by which he btained witness that he was righteous, God testifying of his gifts: and by it he being dead yet speaketh.—HEB. 14: 4.

But this explanation does not satisfy the uninformed and the hypercritical; for such, they say, is not the ordinary experience of mankind. To unbelief human life is an enigma, death a rayless mystery. In this view, which claims to be philosophical, the career of life is painfully wrong, and destitute of meaning. It wanders into deepening gloom without the skill to extricate itself. Its only relief is in the vague notion that in the progress of the ages the miseries of life shall be lessened, and a happier state of things evolve itself out of the existing chaos. But this is the best that can be said of it.

Such, in brief, is the popular skepticism which has its roots in the alienation of the heart from God, and is captivated by any invention which will keep conscience quiet, and draw a mask over eternity. It glides without a pause into materialism—a turning of the theory of evolution upside down, and thereby pushing a well established theory of development into an unsupported and redundant speculation.

With all its dexterity in usurping the place of conscious Divinity, it is utterly incapable of taking a single step beyond the present state of existence. It is barred out of the world to come by its own limitations. Its developments cannot possibly be foreseen. Only when they become manifest can they be known, and thenceforward become historical. The present life is, therefore, an enigma to those who adopt the extreme theory, because the absolute conditions of their own notions arrest them at the moment of death. Nothing beyond the grave touching man's nature can be evolved by them, and hence the arrest is laid upon their own moral and spiritual being—a fatal and inexorable arrest—a barrier which is heaven high and deep as hell. Its unhappy advocates are logical when they push their favorite theory to its legitimate conclusion; and the unknowable is a name which they are compelled to adopt when they renounce the knowledge of the ever-living Creator, and block up the sources of information which they might have followed into the light. It is not strange, therefore, that they call life an enigma and death an inscrutable mystery, or in outspoken phrase, annihilation.

We have to do with man and his future. If he is not complete, if he is not the end of a series, there is occasion for the profoundest concern about his future. If he is the end of a series, then what we call death is his natural and legitimate end, and the whole extinction of developments from protoplasm to the complex being called man. If he is not the end of a series, then by the philosophy of evolution man must die in order to make way for the introduction of the next development. And the next shall be the last: the man renewed in the righteousness and holiness of the Truth, after the pattern of Him that created him. This prophecy finds an echo in our breasts when we cherish hopes of the future which have the hue of delightful anticipations, and that are sometimes the only spur to exertion, and the only citadel amidst disaster and defeat, within which we gather up our remaining resources to renew the conflict.

This hope survives in the midst of successive changes; and it often attempts to cross the silent boundary of life, to speculate about the regions beyond, and even constructs a theory of the future life, giving to it the imaginings that correspond with the pleasures and passions of the life that now is. The springs of such inventions are hidden in our spiritual nature, which is indestructible. And every system of philosophy is false, and all argument is fallacious, which are attempted to be constructed upon any idea of human nature that leaves out a just and consistent consideration of the longings and aspirations of the race universal after the enjoyments of a state of futurity.

Many able thinkers pronounce the atheistic bias of evolution ephemeral because it is partial, for its incompleteness is seen in ignoring some of the indestructible hopes and sentiments of human nature. Its narrowness is at once detected when it conveys us to the verge where all men cry for light, and tries to escape by pronouncing life an enigma which is insoluble, and death a mystery which is unfathomable.

A true and legitimate evolution, as we have seen, forecasts another grand and perhaps final efflorescence in the series, giving to these prophecies in our nature a complete fulfillment in another state of existence. This is not a visionary conclusion, but a logical deduction from the premises that must lie at the foundation of any system of philosophy which requires that all the parts which constitute the essence or the substance of related things, must be accounted for. That is a pretentious theory which arrogantly claims pre-eminence, and yet leaves in limbo the enigmas which it pretends to solve, and mysteries which it should explain, or at least make rational.

Now what does the whole non-theistic drift of this philosophy amount to? As touching Christianity it casts its influence against it, and against any plan of relief, or hint of cure. It encourages not a solitary hope for the present, and sheds no ray upon yonder shoreless ocean.

But what we want to know is how to escape the evils of the present, and how to kindle an undying hope for the future. What we need is not speculation in philosophy, but the plain reason of things, and God to dwell in them all, a God to dictate to Nature as its ruler, and a spirit in man to which God imparts his Spirit. That spirit makes immortality an article of belief, then instills a consciousness of its truth, and finally broadens it into a personal experience.

When this philosophy shall be accepted (towards which the debate is tending), it will soar above the physical environment which now cramps it and materializes it. It will ascend into the spiritual. It will expatiate over realms above physical nature. It will find its true expansion in the supernatural. Even while dwelling in its earthly environment, it is preparing for the house not made with hands.

Thus the enigma of life is solved, and the mysteries of death cleared away. The life is dedicated to nobler aims,

and death is the door of entrance into life eternal. The
fancied enigmas are brushed away with the rubbish of a
false philosophy. The distrust which is born of ignorance
will give place to confidence; and bondage to the objects
of sense will give place to the liberty of heirship in the
spiritual realm.

What a grand idea is this, yet so simple that it is easily
understood, and so comprehensive that there is a place
for everything and all souls in it.

This philosophy disentangles the perplexities which
are evolving from the violent efforts to shut God out of
His Universe, which, like the troubled sea, casts up mire
and dirt, instead of reflecting the cloudless heaven above
it. Immediately upon lifting the gaze above the leaden
waters there appears the simplicity of divine truth, with
pure and noble ideas of righteousness and duty. The
Gospel will appear to be the healer of nature's wounds;
and all its requirements and blessings will be seen to be
consistent with the state of man, and the intellectual and
moral laws which are discernible by the light of nature.

That Gospel in the final philosophy will be accepted as
scientific as well as religious. The conclusions of science
which prove the permanent transmission of hereditary
qualities, at once attests the degeneracy of human nature,
out of which grows the baleful fruit of sins and transgres-
sions. And there remains only the infliction of the penalty,
which is also a deduction of the same science that proves
to us the inflexibility of law and its retributions.

What can possibly be more cheering than to know that

all the penalties of human guilt growing out of the hereditary transmission of a corrupt nature are absolutely borne away by the intervention of ONE who is able to do it in His own person: and that the clearance of every soul is already ordained like an acquittal in a court of justice, upon the simple condition of putting the whole case into the hands of an all-prevailing Advocate and Intercessor.

And this is the imperishable distinction of the Word of God spoken or written, that it continues to re-echo around the world. Hence, it is called the Word of Life. He that came down from heaven to whom God gave all power in heaven and on earth, said to his disciples. "The words that I speak unto you, they are spirit and they are life." The life which he meant was life eternal: for Christ said in his prayer to the Father. " I have given unto them the word which thou gavest me:" and to these words he attached a knowledge of divine things which being received into the heart conveyed the gift of everlasting life. as the Son also said, " This is life eternal that they should know Thee the only true God. and Jesus Christ whom thou hast sent."

Every lover of the Lord Jesus Christ earnestly desires to imbibe the spirit which He manifested in His intercessory prayer from which these words are taken. Their meaning was better understood after the divine Speaker rose from the dead, when it was perceived that a higher operation of law came within the field of human observation. even as when the astronomer discovers a planet which man has never seen before. It has been shining unknown to men and rolling onward in conformity to all nature's laws. So Christ's rising from the dead was no miracle as in any sense contrary to the laws of nature, but as one of a vast series spreading over a field hitherto unexplored by men; even as Hershel's telescope pierced beyond the veil known as the Milky Way, and discovered stars in the profound depths beyond it which were moving onward in harmony with the other heavenly bodies that ever roll in unison with the planetary system around the supreme centre of the seen and unseen Universe. No astronomer had ever looked upon those stars before, yet they had existed through the unrecorded past. When they swung across the vision of men they deranged not the harmony of the spheres. When Christ rose from the dead he created no disturbance of the laws of nature, but was a glorious efflorescence evolved by all the prophecies, the first fruit of them that slept in the dust of the earth. No shock, therefore, was given to the revolutions of nature. A divine harmony prevailed, and joined the melodies of nature to the anthem which completed the oratorio of the Universe, the prelude to which began at the Creation when the morning stars sang together.

This is the order of nature, for " that was not first which was spiritual, but that which is natural, and afterward that which is spiritual ; for the first man was of the earth earthy, the second man is the Lord from heaven. And as we have borne the image of the earthy, we shall also bear the image of the heavenly. Flesh and blood cannot inherit the kingdom of God. Behold I show you a mystery; we shall all be changed in a moment, in the twinkling of an eye." And the change shall be effected at a word; the voice of the archangel shall resound through the habitations of the dead.

Then another word shall be uttered, a note of triumph— "Death is swallowed up in victory. Oh, Death, where is thy sting! Oh, Grave, where is thy victory!"

Another word must be spoken. It is the word of final discrimination. The Old testament utters it :* "Many of them that sleep in the dust of the earth shall awake, some to everlasting life, and some to shame and everlasting contempt." The New testament utters it:† "So shall it be at the end of the world: the angels shall come forth, and sever the wicked from among the just." The Heavenly Messenger proclaims it, as reported by the evangelist John, in a discourse which harmonizes with the truth and the theory I am now anxious to make plain and conclusive: "My Father is working; so also am I." How did the Father work? "He spake, and it was done: He commanded, and it stood fast." How did the Son work? He had just said to a cripple, lying helpless and friendless at Bethesda's pool, "Rise, take up thy bed and walk." The man was sent home cured not by a sign, not by a touch, but by a word. Our Lord's comment was: "Marvel not at this" (that is, the power of the word that healed the impotent man, or the authority that the Son hath to execute judgment), ‡ "Marvel not at this: for the hour is coming, in the which all that

* Dan. 12:2.   † Matt. 13:0.   ‡ John 5:27—29.

are in the graves shall hear his voice, and shall come forth: they that have done good, unto the resurrection of life; and they that have done evil, unto the resurrection of the judgment."

This is the final word. This is the last discrimination that can take place. After which comes the final act of allotment. It is the entrance upon the awards of eternity. It is retribution which follows when the scheme of salvation comes to an end by its own limitation. For the scheme of salvation proceeds upon an expedient to save the guilty from deserved penalty. It provides a substitute who bears the penalty in behalf of all who believe in it and accept it :* " Being justified freely by his grace through the redemption that is in Christ Jesus. "

That life of perfect obedience and that death of infinite suffering made up a redundant righteousness which should forever silence doubt. As it is written : " Where sin abounded, grace doth much more abound; that as sin reigned unto death even so should grace reign through righteousness unto eternal life by Jesus Christ our Lord."†

This is the final word; because it is the Word of the Lord which endureth forever. And this is the Word which by the Gospel is proclaimed everywhere. Christ preached it till the Cross hushed the divine accents of love; and then breaking the silence of the tomb He told the blissful story with new illustrations drawn from the unseen world, and led His followers up to behold as in a mirror the glory of the Lord, that they should be changed

---

* Rom. 3:24.   † Rom. 5, 20, 21.

into the same image "from glory to glory as by the Spirit of the Lord." Then he went up to speak the word of intercession before the great white Throne, while they went forth to speak the Word of reconciliation in the ears of men. He spoke by the voice of prophets. He spoke by the voice of apostles. The prophets and apostles are dead; but though dead they are yet speaking. Their successors rise and speak to each generation. They disappear, and yet speak; for the word is endowed with inextinguishable life. It resounds through both Testaments: "Unto you, O men I call, and my voice is unto the sons of men." New heralds come, recruits swell the ranks of the ministry, and they take up the word: "We are ambassadors for Christ, as though God did beseech you by us; we pray you in Christ's stead be ye reconciled to God. For He hath made him who knew no sin to be sin for us; that we might be made the righteousness of God in him."

Such is the Word of reconciliation, and those that speak it. Every one can proclaim it. Let him that heareth say, Come! And they that hear shall live.

Precisely such is the Gospel in its provision of salvation. Its benefits begin in time. It clears up all enigmas as it goes onward. It makes the track of life luminous; and there is no mystery in death except in the sense that an impenetrable veil hangs between us and those who have gone before. Sometimes the veil is parted for a moment, and we catch a glimpse which transfixes us; and we bear upon our faces for a time the lustre which it kindles.

But the vision is transient—for we are to walk by faith here:—yet the voices which spoke to us in the air we breathe are not silenced since they re-echo in our ears. They are the voices speaking from within the veil to all ears that are disposed to listen to the words of everlasting life. Though we call them dead, they are yet speaking. The Book which contains this final philosophy possesses this living power. Its words, therefore, are living words. The faith it imparts is a living faith. The expectation it inspires is a blessed hope, because it looks for the coming of the great God even our Savior Jesus Christ.

Again. The whole system of Christianity reveals itself as tarrying awhile on this planet to establish its beginnings. Thence it rises into the heavens. How brief its beginning,—the length of a mortal life! How simple its provisions,—a little child can embrace them!

How unspeakably important then is the Word! The messenger of God, the eternal Son assumed our nature that He might utter God's Word, as well as die for human guilt: and the word thus spoken was thenceforth never to die out of the air of this world. It was to sound forth from human lips, and be written upon human hearts. "Ye are my witnesses," said the Word of God. "Ye are our epistles," said St. Paul, "known and read of all men."

The Word therefore both spoken and written is to continue in the world. It vitalizes all the laws of nature or inscribes Deity upon them all, and gives completion to them all. Its inscriptions are never to fade out, because they are written not with ink but with the Spirit of the living God. The finger of death may be laid upon the lips that spoke the Word; but it shall continue to resound. Its vitality may even be increased when the witness departs; the testimony detached from earthly surroundings is approved and verified especially in the person of God's faithful herald who " BEING DEAD YET SPEAKETH."

I have given you, my respected hearers, a sketch of the final philosophy, not intended to be analytical or argumentative, but designed to touch salient points, to disclose connections otherwise hidden, to catch glimpses of the heavenly heights, to convince us that God reigns in all things, is the operator of all law, and out of feeble agencies evolves the mightiest, redeeming fallen man, taking all superhuman obstacles out of the way of his salvation, stooping to him in his helplessness even as a father pitieth; and then gathering all the saved into one vast family, the inheritance of saints in light. And all conducted in conformity to law observed in its precept or suffered in its penalty by a Substitute who was almighty to save sinners, that the law might be magnified and made honorable from the outer rim of heaven to the depths of hell,—an expedient of mercy unheard of in heaven's legislation; but when known it excites the highest adoration of those who see God in the person of the co-eternal Son taking our nature upon Him that He might fight our battles for us, conquer our last enemy, Death, and destroy the works of the devil, and then go

through the suffering of death that we might live—
the anguish of the Cross being infinitely deepened by the
transference of human guilt to Him; for He bore our sins
and sorrows in his own body on the tree.

The pertinence of this outline will appear, when I say
that it represents Dr. Geary's philosophical views, and in
substance his theological also. It serves to remind us
how our lamented friend and counsellor kept abreast
with the advance of thought, and broadened his views of
divine truth by examining current questions. The
subtilty with which he unraveled the intricacies of a
problem, and the ease which marked his analysis of
parts and their reconstruction into harmonious propor-
tions, were a demonstration of the reasonableness of his
conclusions that showed the capacity of a superior mind,
polished and enlarged by culture which embraced the entire intellectual, moral and spiritual nature of the man.
We cite him as an example of the comprehensive education which is confined to no utilitarian scheme, and that
leaves no department of human nature unimproved, and
no region of investigation unexplored which man is
qualified to enter.

My respected hearers, whose minds are disciplined to
impartial discriminations by the study of causes and the
observation of phenomena, will expect me to do justice
to the memory of their peer in perspicacity and erudition;
and I, therefore, hesitate not to say that he maintained
the value of metaphysical studies as an indispensable

department of a liberal education. He deplored the trend given towards materialism by the intense activities of the age, which have warped also our systems of education and biased our literary judgments. A few popular writers who have fallen under the dominion of matter and force, have labored with ability to strengthen the trend towards materialism, impelled by their undisguised contempt for all studies which they consider above nature, and therefore illusive and unprofitable. The influence which these theorists have acquired by carrying their studies of physical nature beyond all precedent explorers, has invested their speculations with an unwarranted authority; which has placed the advocates of metaphysical studies in a lateral position; but wherever the advocate may be, the foundation is unshaken. It rests in the nature of the human spirit and the absolute claim of the mind to be educated in every part into a consistent and well proportioned personality. This embraces the cultivation of the spiritual capacities, to be prosecuted for their intrinsic worth, heightened by the consideration that these spiritual capabilities are the gifts of God wherein we most resemble Him.

Our Memorial would be decapitate if it should fail to shed light upon this groundwork of all his reasonings, and the system of philosophy thus evolved. It could not be satisfactory to his intimate friends if his memorialist should omit to mention the acuteness of his understanding through which he discerned the relations of ideas, from whence ascending through the dry light of

abstract principles into the regions of applied science
and the phenomena of nature, everything both ideal and
practical fell into an orderly and consecutive adjustment
in his own mind; and when occasion justified it, he ex-
cited the admiration of listeners as he set forth these
principles by way of deduction and induction, and
showed their relations upon the field of thought which
was laid clearly open before us, and expounded with the
skill of a master the responsibilities of man both to his
kind and to his God.

Positive doctrines and affirmative ideas are among
the most precious fruit of such a process of reasoning.
It is the outgrowth of an aphorism of Lord Bacon:

"Let no one . . . think or maintain that a man can search too
far or be too well studied in the book of God's Word, or in the book
of God's Works—divinity or philosophy—but rather let men endeavor
an endless progress or proficiency in both ; only let them beware that
they apply both to charity and not to arrogance ; to use and not to
ostentation ; and again, that they do not mingle or confound these
learnings together."

Undoubtedly the author of the Inductive method intended to caution the student against regarding the book
of nature as a completed guide: for if it were it would
therefore supersede any occasion for the book of God's
Word.

Dr. Geary's intellectual habitude was in conformity
with this aphorism thus explained : and the sum and re-
sult upon his character and teaching was an expansion

into the broadest regions of liberal thought and sentiment. This was not the stifling philosophy which confines its culture to this world alone, and nurses the vague speculations which are no better than the extinction of the future state, and consequently the annihilation of all hope beyond the grave.

He took delight to the last in expatiating over these regions of thought. Not long ago as he laid down Professor Diman's Theistic Argument, he exclaimed, " It is all there—the argument is complete. God is high as heaven above the feeble intellects of man." He rejoiced to see more sharply with the eye of sense God's footsteps on the earth, and His signature in the skies.

But I should fail to do justice to this part of our subject if I should omit to say that these excursions into the realms of nature were logical supports of his religious views, which were evangelical. The inspired Word taught him the fallen state of man; the atoning work of Christ, who makes God the Father known ; the necessity of being renewed by the Holy Spirit; and of faith, repentance and obedience in order to be saved; the immortality of the soul; the eternal retributions of the judgment both to the wicked and the righteous. He held the liberty of choice, which implies human accountability for rejecting or accepting salvation, while he vindicated the sovereignty of God in the whole work of redemption; and brought man a helpless sinner to the footstool of mercy, humble, penitent, grateful. He saw the God of revelation, a sovereign in the works of grace as well as of nature, and found far less difficulty in this view of the problems of evil than in any other method of explaining them. He would, therefore, be called a Calvinist by those who make theological distinctions. He maintained these views with signal ability, while he shunned a dogmatic and controversial spirit. His disposition was catholic and fraternal. The tenacity with which he held these doctrinal views and the exceeding clearness in which he apprehended them as the only rational and consistent interpretation of the Scriptures, did not make him exclusive or impatient with his brethren who entertained different views. He adopted Augustine's rule: " In things trivial, let there be liberty; in essentials, unity; in all things, charity." He deplored the sectarian divisions of the Church on earth; and was always eager to join in any demonstration of visible union. You remember his earnest prayers that all Christians might become one in visible fellowship as well as one in spirit. I remember them as offered on different public occasions. Dr. Geary reached the conclusion that the want of fellowship and comity among the different sects were the greatest hindrances to the spread of the Gospel, especially in the new settlements of our country. "I believe in the Holy Catholic Church, the communion of saints " is still in the creed of Christendom; and if it were practised it would give a vast power to Christian sentiment, and bear with great weight upon all the interests of mankind. It would instantly suppress some evils and establish some reforms for which we are separately contending in vain. And is it not time before God and the world for all denominations to hold their creeds and ordinances in subordination to the broader generalizations of the Gospel? This union army is increasing in drill and power, and the day of its triumph shall come when the Saviour's prayer shall be answered, "That they all may be one in us, that the world may believe that Thou didst send Me." Then Dr. Geary will be remembered as an earnest advocate of Union in this part of the Lord's Kingdom.

These broad church sentiments, Dr. Geary held, were consistent with his Presbyterian theology, and ecclesiastical relations. Hence, his preaching abounded with the fullness and the freeness of salvation, and the tender of unconditional fellowship to all of every name who love our Lord Jesus Christ in sincerity.

Though Dr. Geary was a man of extensive learning, and capable of the profoundest research, yet he never paraded his erudition. He brought the beaten oil into the sanctuary ; he broke the alabaster box, and the name of Jesus was as fragrance poured forth. He extracted the honey out of the rock. But he learned the divine art at the feet of his Master. He wondered at the gracious words that fell from the Saviour's lips ; then he imbibed his spirit, and preached as Jesus and the Apostles did. His sermons were able expositions of saving and sanctifying truth. They were addressed to the conscience and the heart. They were scriptural. They proclaimed salvation on the authority of God, as a herald would publish the proclamation of his sovereign. He appealed much to reason that it might apprehend, but more to faith, that it might trust, and to gratitude that it might love and adore. From general truths he deduced pungent and special applications, and often dealt with current occasions of discourse, to the delight and edification of his hearers : but always basing his appeals upon the written Word.

Dr. Geary never forgot that the efficacy of preaching depended upon the Holy Spirit, who works with those that honor Him with their dependence, trust and expectation. Such preaching sows the seed of the kingdom ; and the harvest shall ripen in due time. The preacher shall disappear : BUT HE BEING DEAD YET SPEAKETH.

On communion seasons Dr. Geary was in his element. His devotional spirit spread from heart to heart. He was transformed as he dwelt upon the scene with Jesus in the midst, and heard the word that the Master spoke, "With desire have I desired to eat this passover with you." He went up into the holy mount as Moses did with the elders, as it is written, "They saw the God of Israel ; and there was under his feet a pavement of sapphire stone, and the body of heaven in its clearness. And the glory of the Lord rested upon the Mount."

In Brother Geary's hands the sacrament was a symbol of the Lamb slain ; and a prophecy of his return. Yet he came from the mountains of myrrh and the garden of spices and the sealed fountains, and refreshed the souls that longed for the Saviour's presence and his communion gifts. I remember one occasion when dear Brother

Geary lost sight of surroundings, and poured out his soul in praise and prayer : and he communed with his Saviour as friend talks with friend. It was a solemn and affecting scene, never to be forgotten.

Profoundly impressed with the sin and want of human hearts and the all-sufficiency of Christ to cleanse and comfort them, Brother Geary's preaching has ever shown the depth and power of his convictions. The soul and its salvation, Christ and his redeeming grace, were to him vivid realities. They gave tone to his voice, and his words were full of earnestness, tenderness, and love. His voice we shall hear no more : BUT HE IS YET SPEAKING.

When Mr. Geary's ministerial life began, the influence of the ministry was more generally felt in society : it was more conspicuous ; and the clergyman was held, in consequence, in a more sacred or reserved estimate than he is at the present day. Now, he stands nearer the level of other professional men. The teacher, the physician, the writer for the press, the lawyer, the lecturer—mingle their influences with the currents that control society or attract its attention. In all respects but one, this change is perhaps not injurious : and that one is the tendency, especially in literary circles, to underrate and put aside the legitimate power of the pulpit. But no broad-minded minister of the gospel would desire any influence which he does not deserve ; while at the same time he feels the importance of securing the respect which is due to his position as a teacher of religion. He is bound to " magnify his office " for the sake of others. He must claim for it what his Master authorized when He instituted the ministry. He said to the incumbents, "He that receiveth you receiveth Me, and he that receiveth Me receiveth Him that sent Me." He attached a solemn distinction to the office and the incumbent in these words and others of the same nature. It was the respect that was due to the bearer of a message of infinite importance to the whole human race; and it is impossible to treat the messenger with contempt without reflecting upon the God who sends the message.

No one will dispute the principle which underlies this remark; and there remains the suggestion of congruity which demands that there should be a character of consistency in the ambassador who brings the terms of pardon and reconciliation. When this consistency is wanting it is impossible to treat the incumbent with the respect which is due to his office. And since the office itself is so elevated, should not the incumbent be conformed to it and transformed by it? And as the communications through it are so comprehensive as embracing time and eternity, and yet so minute as to enter into and regulate our daily lives, is it not a very reasonable expectation that the man who occupies it should present a fair example of the advantages which his own message proposes to others? Surely the message includes the harmonious development of the intellectual and moral nature; and, in short, the culture of manhood which presents to every observer a symmetrical character.

Our friend never claimed an exorbitant respect for his office, and he put forth no ghostly prerogatives ; nor did he ever claim for himself any regard which was not due to any educated and honorable man. His intercourse with the public and his contemporaries in the professions will amply sustain this opinion. There is that sense of congruity in faithfulness and competency, that yields respectful deference.

This gives me the opportunity to recall some characteristics of our departed friend. He stands before you a stately figure with a countenance expressive of wisdom and benevolence, giving the beholder a striking impression of manly dignity. His air attracted confidence ; his sincerity was a pledge that it would not be betrayed. He was slow to speak when the occasion demanded reflection ; and his words dropped from his lips in the orderly arrangement which none but a well trained intellect is capable of. And when the theme aroused his intellectual powers, his discourse was the manifest expression of a mind which penetrated into the subject, and comprehended the whole; and yet so discriminating and analytical was it, that no conditions escaped him; and therefore, his conclusion was the essence of a complete and satisfactory survey.

His wise and sagacious views answered the expectations which his impressive appearance awakened. And it was his happy experience to justify the anticipations of his admirers. Among these were the extremes of society. He had the faculty to entertain and instruct the people

whose education had been limited, while his erudition and
other accomplishments placed him in the front rank of
educated and professional men. These qualities shone
forth in the debates which take place in deliberative assem-
blies as well as in the class-room and the limited circle of
social life.

He was simple, sincere and unobtrusive. Though
grave and reserved among strangers he was not cold, un-
social or haughty; but sympathetic and considerate, having
all the instincts of a gentleman. Among congenial friends
he was tender, unreserved, and affectionate, often gratifying his literary taste by quotations from classical and
dramatic authors, yet never forgetting what was becoming
in a man and a Christian. He was ever ready to help any
one who was in distress at the sacrifice of his own ease
and comfort ; and would rather be the victim of impos-
ture than to turn a deaf ear to the stranger. He gave
without humiliating the recipient. He was a generous
helper of his brethren. He welcomed them to his hospi-
table home. He counselled them, and judged their weak-
nesses charitably. And when compelled to differ from
them, his manliness retained their respect, and his kind-
ness their affection. He was condescending without the
affectation of superiority.

The basis of this character was integrity, purified and
informed by the grace of God. It is this foundation upon
which rises the structure of manhood that abides forever,
because it is well pleasing in the sight of God. The great
poet of Paradise thus expresses it:

This is true glory and repute, when God
Looking on the earth, with approbation marks
The just man, and divulges him through Heaven
To all his angels, who with true applause
Recount his praise.

God prepared him to be one of the pioneers of enlightened civilization in these distant territories. The
founders of American civilization on the Pacific Coast
were not the seekers after gold who plowed up the glitter-
ing sands or pulverized the auriferous quartz, but the stan-
dard-bearers of true progress, the pioneers of liberty, learning, and religion. Various motives influenced them;
brilliant prospects allured them: the command to march
like a bugle-call was heard in their tabernacles: and with
love of adventure was mingled love of country and a splen-
did courage. If the pioneers had flourished in the times
of the ancient mythology, they would have been celebrated
as heroes, and their leaders as demi-gods. And truly they
needed political intelligence and wisdom from on high to
mold the elements, combine the powers, and shape the
destinies of the new States.

The real founders of States are not warriors at the
head of marshalled hosts: but the leaders of pacific armies
who raise the standard of liberty, education and religion.
We who are daily enjoying the fruit which they planted
are apt to forget their sufferings and self-denials. And in
this direction Dr. Geary's patriotic services are much
overlooked.

But he did not court this species of renown, however honorable. His grateful fellow-citizens sought to confer upon him the highest distinctions within the power of the State to bestow. On one of these occasions, he emphatically expressed his determination to live and die in the ministry of Christ. Let us continue to look at him in the light he chose. We see therein his completer life as a minister of the Gospel.

The best trained minds in the world are either open disciples of Christ or believers in the truth of Christianity. They aid in supporting its schools and churches and its aggressive movements upon the hosts of ignorance and sin, or in a less pronounced way they advocate its moral principles and its civilizing influences.

The profoundest students of history are the men who trace the causes of a nation's progress and bring their effects to light; and these are the men who proclaim the power of the Gospel to educate and civilize not a few favored ones only, but the entire mass of the nation.

These conclusions are just without abbreviation, when applied to the settlement and early progress of a country. And if true greatness consists in the measure of a man's usefulness to his generation, it is all intensified, when that man stands in the integrity of his virtue and the will and accomplishment of his usefulness as a pioneer. Now this conclusion being accepted, there remains the superadded power and influence of the reigning purpose, which is the laying foundations of religious and educational institutions in the community, and the upbailding of a divine nature in the individual character.

In this comprehensive view Edward R. Geary stands in the front rank of the world's benefactors. Others of the pioneers stand with him, whom we honor without abridging their claims; but it belongs to this occasion to speak of him whose memory fills our thoughts and our hearts.

The applause of contemporaries is sometimes ill-founded through the bias of prejudice or local colorings; but taking the ground upon which the judgment of history is formed, we hesitate not to predict that posterity will crown Edward R. Geary as one among the first of the patriotic heroes of the Pacific North West, and raise his spotless effigy in her Pantheon. In the meantime his living statue is carried within our hearts; and his living words resound in our ears; for though gone far beyond our ken, he is speaking still.

A great sorrow has overshadowed us. It enshrouds the family that unconsciously listens for a footstep that will never return; it drapes the domestic altar upon which the fire of affection shall be replenished until the light it creates shall mingle with the lustre of the endless day. It descends upon the church like a funeral pall: it saddens the brethren who shall not see his face again until they ascend where he is.

A whole generation that has passed away on this coast paid him the homage of their confidence which his worth and fidelity deserved; and now their successors offer their

54

tribute of regard and reverence. Friendship overflows
with grateful offerings bedewed with recollections that
melt into tears. Love inscribes no epitaph, erects no
monument. Its reminiscences are a perpetual memorial,
its monument is the heart ; and we shall hear that voice
intoning no sorrow. for it speaketh of memories now hal-
lowed, and of hope that beckons into immortality.

He died without being able to tell us what his personal
experience of the end of this life was, or how his life-long
views compared with the approaching realities, and what
the landscape was as he gazed with nearing vision upon
the scenery of heaven; but there remains the broader sat-
isfaction in the testimony of his witnesses, who are the
ignorant he has enlightened, the suffering he has relieved.
the bereaved he has consoled, the dying he has guided to
the river's brink, where he dispersed the gloom by diffus-
ing the light he himself saw shining upon the farther
shore, and by which he kindled the watch-fires upon the
promontories of his own life abounding in consecrated
labors; and we gather from them what his last words
would have been; for by these HE YET SPEAKETH.

And what is he saying? His whole life is resonant
with instruction. Like a grand organ, though its har-
monies are ever and anon disturbed by the finger of discord.
(the imperfection that still lurks in our nature), yet when
touched by the Master's hand, responds in rich and re-
sounding melody, so the voice that speaks to us now
reiterates its lessons on the keys that are pure and true,

in the tone that gathers solemnity by its transmission to us from the unseen world. Blessed are they that shall heed the lessons.

1. He speaks to the friends of higher education. We have not many among us who could place the principles of advanced culture upon the erudite and philosophical principles which he so ably maintained. He was himself a bright example of continuous and fruitful study. He forestalled the rust of age by friction of thought and investigation, and he loved profound inquiry, and followed it with the fervor of youth and the tenacity of mature life.

His association with the managers of our State University was doubtless an intellectual spur; while we have the evidence that they regarded him as an efficient co-operator in the work of moulding an institution which should embrace the substantial principles evolved from the experience of the past, and the approved progress of the present. His noble example will be a living inspiration to his successors. Though he has become invisible, his memory will be cherished, not only for his wise counsels among his brethren who were aided by his wide and varied culture and experience, but he will continue to be admired for the purity of his character, and the genial qualities which he displayed in fraternal regard and sympathy.

2. He yet speaketh in example to young men, especially to students who are in pursuit of a liberal education. He began early to shape his course for a comprehensive

culture. His thirst for knowledge was unslaked by his reading, although he eagerly perused all the books that came within his reach. No doubt his ideas about the advantages of a college course were limited; but they were influential enough to carry him through all difficulties; and they were not trivial. His struggles made him strong. They were steel to the flint that rekindled his purpose and made it inflexible. The habits so formed accrued to his character, and made its principles firm as granite.

He passed with high honor through the course in Jefferson College, class of 1834, standing abreast of men who afterwards achieved great distinction in the professions, himself inferior to none in contemporary fame if he had remained in the Atlantic States. His success shows that literary scholarship and generous culture does not depend upon studying a multitude of branches, but upon the tested and conscious acquisition of the essential studies which constitute a liberal education. The colleges of fifty years ago supported their polished arches upon the symmetrical columns dedicated to mathematics, classics, literature and history, physics, natural science, intellectual and moral philosophy. In the modern multiplicity of studies and subdivisions of branches the tendency is in the direction of miscellaneous overloading; and there is the danger of missing the true culture and discipline of the mind. A fundamental idea in liberal culture is the training of the mind for its own sake. Independent thought and sound reasoning, comprehensive views and liberal sentiments are the reward of a symmetrical development of all the faculties. Cultivated faculties are the polished instruments of a well balanced mind and an enlightened conscience. They raise the spirit to self-command and a prudent self-confidence.

The rewards of patient industry and improvement of every faculty were crowned with consecration to God our Saviour, in the person of the young and ardent Geary. His manly spirit and broad sympathies were disciplined by his struggles; and he always sought to assist and strengthen young people who were seeking the advantages of education. I can mention only one instance. A gentleman of high standing and acknowledged scholarship wrote to me: " It makes me indescribably sad. Dr. Geary was my best friend in Oregon, and I cherish his memory in my heart; and as I write and think of the past, I can scarcely restrain my tears."

3. He speaks to the rising ministry. With amazing emphasis he would say: Preach the Gospel. Maintain the honor of the Lord Jesus Christ. Do not underrate the sufficiency of Revelation. It is God's Word, inspired by his Spirit. It contains the only hope for the world to come, in the intercession of the once crucified Redeemer. Be faithful ambassadors of God to a rebellious race, while you maintain the character of true manhood in incorruptible integrity, unblemished reputation, unflinching support of truth, virtue and goodness, and identification with the Lord Jesus Christ. May your record be that of the apostles: "Our rejoicing is this, the testimony of

our conscience that in simplicity and godly sincerity, not with fleshly wisdom but by the grace of God, we have had our conversation in the world."

4. He speaks to disciples. He seems to say: " I stir up your pure minds by way of remembrance. Be faithful unto death, and ye shall receive the crown of life."

5. He speaks to the unconverted. With burning desire he would break the solemn silence if he could, and bid you to flee from the wrath to come : for heaven and hell are realities. But you need not be lost. There is room in the love of God, there is room in heaven for you.

Respected hearers! May you so dwell in the grace of Christ and under the tuition of his Spirit, that your life may be an offering sacred to charity and devotion, that it may be said of it at last,

By it he being dead yet speaketh.

MINUTE OF THE SYNOD OF THE COLUMBIA.

Your Committee on Necrology report the death of one member of our body during the past year, REV. EDWARD R. GEARY, D. D., the father of the Presbytery of Oregon, and one of the fathers of this Synod. He has been called up higher after a life full of years and honors down here. It has been the lot of but few men to fill so many and varied positions in the service of his country, of his church, and of his God, and to fill them so well as Father Geary, as his younger brethren delighted to call him. A many-sided man, he believed that in choosing the holy calling of the Gospel ministry he did not, because he could not, lay aside the sacred privileges, responsibilities and duties of an American citizen. Called of God, through the voice of the people, or their chosen rulers, to positions of public trust outside of the regular line of pulpit and pastoral work, he promptly responded to such claims of duty; and we record with pleasure that when those public services were rendered, he laid his well-earned honors down, and returned to his ministerial work, possessing alike the confidence of Christians and non-professors, as a man who, under all temptations, could be depended upon to stand for and do *the right*. His ability as an expounder of the sacred Scriptures, and as a pulpit orator, as well as his faithful and loving work as a pastor, need no commendation at the hands of his brethren.

But he has gone to his reward; and the record of a faithful and noble life is left for the reading of those who live after him. May the Holy Spirit enable us to follow in the footsteps of the Master, building up the church which our venerable departed brother loved so well.

We extend our heartfelt sympathy to the family of our deceased brother, assuring them of our faith that their and our loss is his eternal gain.

Adopted October 14, 1886.

TRIBUTES.

Dr. Geary Dead.

Edward R. Geary, D.D., one of the most prominent citizens of this city and State, died at his residence in Eugene, last Wednesday evening, Sept. 1, 1886, admired, respected and beloved by all our citizens, and pursuing his duties as pastor of the Presbyterian church, preaching his last sermon only three weeks ago.

His work in behalf of the State University of which he was regent, was effective and untiring, and a great part of the success of that institution is due to his efforts.

Dr. Geary possessed the highest intellectual and moral qualities that made him an ornament to the community. In all good causes to benefit and improve the people he was a leader, and in all cases where he antagonized other men's opinions, he did it so conscientiously, with so much courtesy and toleration, as to win their sincere friendship, and leave a pleasant memory of himself in their minds. In short, he was a grand, good, Christian gentleman.

The Eugene City Guard.

A Good Man Gone.

Rev. E. R. Geary, D.D., one of the ablest divines in the Presbyterian church on the northwest, died the 1st inst. . . Dr. Geary was one of whom nothing but good could be said. His life in its entirety, was devoted to good works, and he had reached a spot in the confidences of men, seldom gained. Trusted by all, beloved by every-one, truly his death leaves a void.

Jacksonville Democrat.

Death in the Ministry.

We are sorry to be under the necessity of announcing the death of Rev. E. R. Geary, D.D., a member of the Presbytery of Oregon, and one of the pioneer ministers of the Presbyterian church on the Pacific Coast. Dr. Geary was a native of Pennsylvania, and a brother of the late Governor of this State, of that name. He was a man of great self-devotion to his work, and stood at the head of the men who at an early date went forth to found churches and schools in far-distant Oregon. He wrought long and well, without the inspiration of near association with his brethren, but with a firm purpose to serve God and his generation, and he has passed away, honored and revered by the men to whom he preached, and by the church to which he was so faithful.

Philadelphia Presbyterian.